Richard Jackson & Katherine Tillotson

THE THREE BILLY GOATS GRUFF

THE **FULL** STORY

A CAITLYN DLOUHY BOOK

Atheneum Books for Young Readers
New York London Toronto Sydney New Delhi

SO...
here are the Brothers Gruff:

Big Billy Goat,

Middle Billy Goat,

and

Little Billy Goat.

They are famous because of a loudmouth
bully boy under a bridge.

Here he is.

He's called Troll

And he thinks the bridge is his.

All his.

The river, too, most likely.

Just look at him:

gnarly,

toes curled around stones,

saplings sprouting

from his head and neck.

And his breath?

Whew!

Now, it happens
that our three billy goats
have chewed and chomped and swallowed up
all the mountain grass on their side of the river.

Still, they are hungry. Beyond the bridge,
over the river, their cousins graze on the mountain opposite,
where enough lush grass grows for everyone. The Brothers Gruff
watch the Cousins Gruff munch-munching away and . . .

well, they are envious.

These cousins are not famous.

They are content.

They have enough.

They want nothing more.

Unlike Big Billy, Middle Billy, and Little Billy,

who want some of that green grass for themselves.

But to get it, they must cross the bridge

where YOU-KNOW-WHO is hiding,

breathing his bilious breath and

MUTT-MUTTERING.

Because Troll, too, is hungry—
fed to the teeth (and what teeth!)
with sticks and mud and green river scum.
He longs for a meal of good goat.

Imagine his mouth-watery joy
when he sees the Gruffs coming his way
down their mountain.

Little Billy first,

then Middle Billy,

and Big Billy last.

Troll hunkers . . . .

and hears . . .

Trip-trap.

    Trip-trap.

That's the sound
of Little Billy's
shiny tiny hoofs
above him:

Trip-trap.

    Trip-trap.

"Aeh!

Who is that tap-tap-tapping
on my bridge?" asks Troll.

"Only I, Little Billy Goat, of the Brothers Gruff,"
says Little Billy, "on my way to see my cousins.
Please let me pass."

"Not before
I gobble you up,
you measly morsel,"
Troll booms from below.

"Wait, wait," says Little Billy.
"My bigger brother Middle Billy
is following just behind.
He is a **mighty meal**
compared to miniscule me."

"I'll eat you both," says Troll.
"I'm **that** hungry."
And he reaches a scaly paw upward
through the boards of the bridge.

But Little Billy scampers past,

just out of Troll's reach.

Once across and over the river,
Little Billy stops for breath,
turns,
and hears . . .

Trip-trap.

TRIP-TRAP.

That's the sound
of not-so-little
Middle Billy's
medium-sized hoofs.

Trip-trap.

TRIP-TRAP.

"Aeh!
Who is that
tap-tap-tapping
on my bridge?"
asks Troll.
(Oh that voice! Like a tornado.)

"Only I, Middle Billy Goat, of the Brothers Gruff,"
Middle Billy says,
"on my way to join my brother
to visit our cousins
on the mountain opposite.
Kindly let me pass."

"Not before I gobble you up,
you meaty modicum,"
Troll booms from below.

"Wait, wait,"
says Middle Billy.
"Our biggest brother, Big Billy,
is following just behind.
He is a meal-worthy mouthful
compared to middling me."

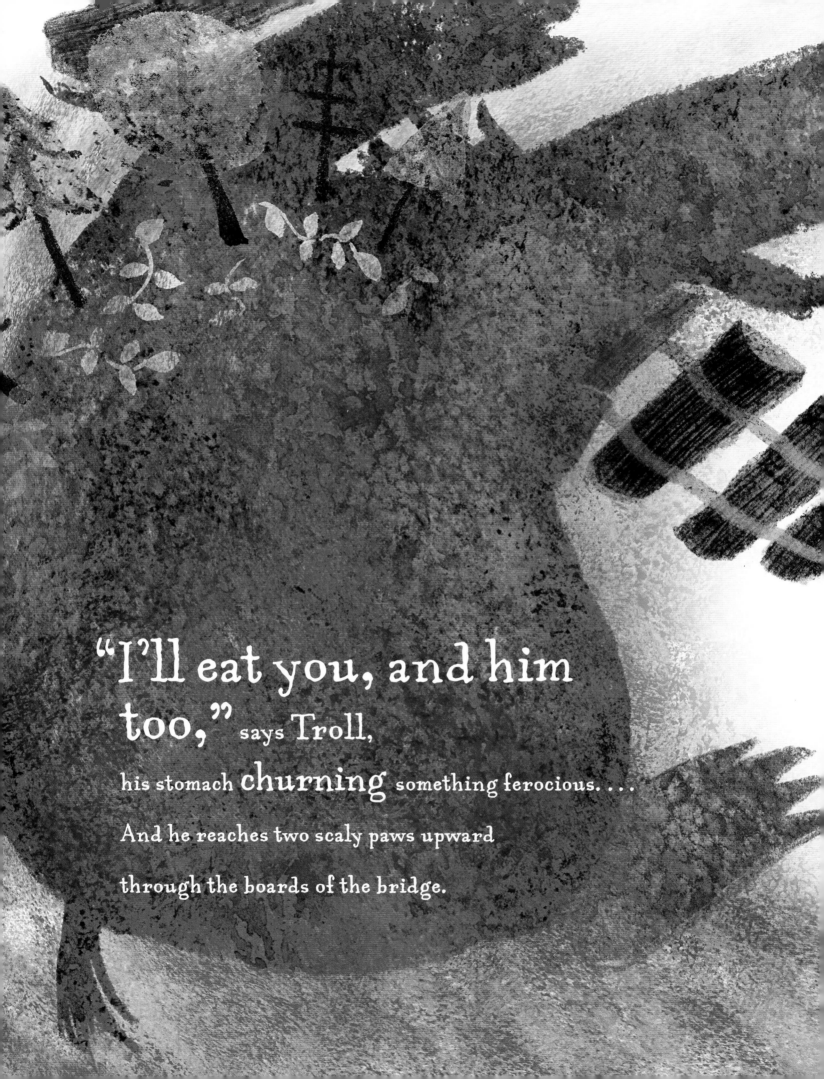

"I'll eat you, and him too," says Troll,

his stomach churning something ferocious....

And he reaches two scaly paws upward

through the boards of the bridge.

But Middle Billy slips-slides past,
just out of Troll's long reach.

Once across and over the river,
Middle Billy stops for breath,
spies his little brother ahead,
hi-hos, and turns to hear . . .

TRIP-TRAP. TRIP-TRAP.

That's the sound of not-at-all-middle-sized
Big Billy's **huge** hoofs.

TRIP-TRAP. TRIP-TRAP.

"Aeh!

Who is that tap-TAP-TAPPING
on my bridge?" asks Troll.
(That voice again—only worse. Like a typhoon.)

"Who do you **think**, Trolly?
It is I, Big Billy Goat, of the Brothers Gruff,"
says Big Billy,
"on my way to join my brothers
and visit our cousins
on the mountain opposite.

Now, let me pass or . . ."

"Or **what**, billy boy?" says Troll.
"No **PLEASE**, no **KINDLY**?
Well, **NO THANK YOU**,
Gruff-stuff."

With that, Troll swings his whole scaly self
up, up, up onto the bridge.

"I will gobble you up, I will, I will,"
Troll bellows.

"Come on, then, bully boy!"
Big Billy roars back,
(just take a look at those two old horns;
 a gander at those four huge hoofs ... Whoa!)
  and then—here's the famous part—

BB boots Troll

sky-**high** into the air,

where Troll has never, **ever** been before.

Uff-da!

Is that his stomach or his mouth mutt-muttering?

"Come on," Big Billy says to
Brother Little and Brother Middle,
and all three skitter up the mountain,
join their Cousins Gruff, and together
share the lush grass as a family.

"Want to hear," Big Billy says to the cousins,
"about our Troll below?" He looks up.
"Or our Troll above?"

"YES!" the cousins say.
They all stop chewing.

"Well...,"
Billy Boy begins.

And so it happens that the story is first told—
the story, like all stories, of Who Wants What . . .
and Do They Get It?

Big Billy has one answer.

Middle Billy has another, even better.

And Little Billy has the best.

At last the Cousins Gruff want something:

"More!" they cry.
"More of that story, please and kindly."

And poor Troll. Does he want more of that story?

Or just a little peace and quiet while he once again settles,
mutt-muttering
for his sticks and mud and green river scum?

In memory of Dick Jackson,
storyteller, mischief-maker, mentor, and friend.

Thank you to Caitlyn Dlouhy, Ann Bobco,
Sonia Chaghatzbanian, and Irene Metaxatos for
all their guidance and support. I would never have
made it across the bridge without them.

—K. T.

Ⓐ ATHENEUM BOOKS FOR YOUNG READERS
An imprint of Simon & Schuster Children's Publishing Division
1230 Avenue of the Americas, New York, New York 10020
Text copyright © 2020 by Richard Jackson
Illustrations copyright © 2020 by Katherine Tillotson
ATHENEUM BOOKS FOR YOUNG READERS is a registered trademark of Simon & Schuster, Inc.
Atheneum logo is a trademark of Simon & Schuster, Inc.
For information about special discounts for bulk purchases, please contact Simon & Schuster
Special Sales at 1-866-506-1949 or business@simonandschuster.com.
The Simon & Schuster Speakers Bureau can bring authors to your live event. For more information
or to book an event, contact the Simon & Schuster Speakers Bureau at 1-866-248-3049 or visit our
website at www.simonspeakers.com.
Jacket design by Irene Metaxatos
The text for this book was set in Aunt Mildred.
Manufactured in China
0620 SCP
First Edition
10 9 8 7 6 5 4 3 2 1
Library of Congress Cataloging-in-Publication Data
Names: Jackson, Richard, 1935-2019, author. | Tillotson, Katherine, illustrator.
Title: Three billy goats Gruff—the FULL story/ Richard Jackson ; Illustrated by Katherine Tillotson.
Description: First edition. | New York : Atheneum Books for Young Readers, [2020] |
"A Caitlyn Dlouhy book." | Summary: Expands on the well-known tale of three clever goat brothers
trying to cross a bridge guarded by a mean and hungry troll.
Identifiers: LCCN 2017043840 | ISBN 9781481415736
(hardcover) | ISBN 9781481415743 (eBook)
Subjects: | CYAC: Fairy tales. | Folklore—Norway.
Classification: LCC PZ8.J178 Thr 2020 |
DDC 398.2 [E]—dc23 LC record available at
https://lccn.loc.gov/2017043840